For my aunty Fiona, for the unbreakable support and laughs x

First U.S. edition 2015

Library of Congress Catalog Card Number 2014939340
ISBN 978-0-7636-7593-6

14 15 16 17 18 19 TLF 10 9 8 7 6 5 4 3 2 1

Printed in Dongguan, Guandong, China

This book was typeset in ACaslon Regular.
The illustrations were done in mixed media.

TEMPLAR BOOKS

an imprint of Candlewick Press
99 Dover Street
Somerville, Massachusetts 02144
www.candlewick.com

GEMMA O'NEILL

MONTY'S MAGNIFICENT MANE

templar books

an imprint of Candlewick Press

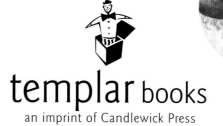

Meet Monty, King of the Jungle.
Monty loves his long, curly,
beautiful mane.

No one else has a mane quite like his.

Monty thinks it's **magnificent**.

"Monty, your mane is gorgeous and shiny and the longest in the jungle," say his friends the meerkats.

Monty likes hearing this very much. So he lets the meerkats play in his lovely mane. . . .

But then they tug and tickle, so Monty rumbles, grumbles,

and rolls . . .

CRASH!

Monty ends up taking a tumble.
Now his mane is dirty
and matted!

The meerkats try to help.
They brush and braid his mane and
decorate it with feathers.

But Monty is **not** amused.

So he shakes

out the braids and feathers . . .

and stomps off to the water hole to check his reflection.

"Monty!" says one little meerkat as he leaves.
"Remember to be careful of the ..."

But Monty has already stomped away.

While admiring his mane at the water hole, Monty sees a little creature in the water.

"My, what a wonderful mane you have," says the creature to Monty.
"In fact, some might say it's magnificent.
Why don't you come a little closer so I can see it better?"

Monty fluffs out his mane and prances closer to his new friend.

He gets closer . . .

and closer . . .

and closer . . .

until . . .

Monty leaps away, but the crocodile
got a big bite of his beautiful mane.
Then the crocodile climbs out of the water.

So Monty runs for home as fast as he can!

But when he gets there, Monty realizes that he's made a **terrible** mistake.
The crocodile has followed him and spotted his friends.

"Meerkats!" snarls the hungry creature.

"My favorite!"

Even though the meerkats mess up Monty's mane sometimes,
he can't let the crocodile eat them!

Monty tosses his mane,
throws back his head . . .

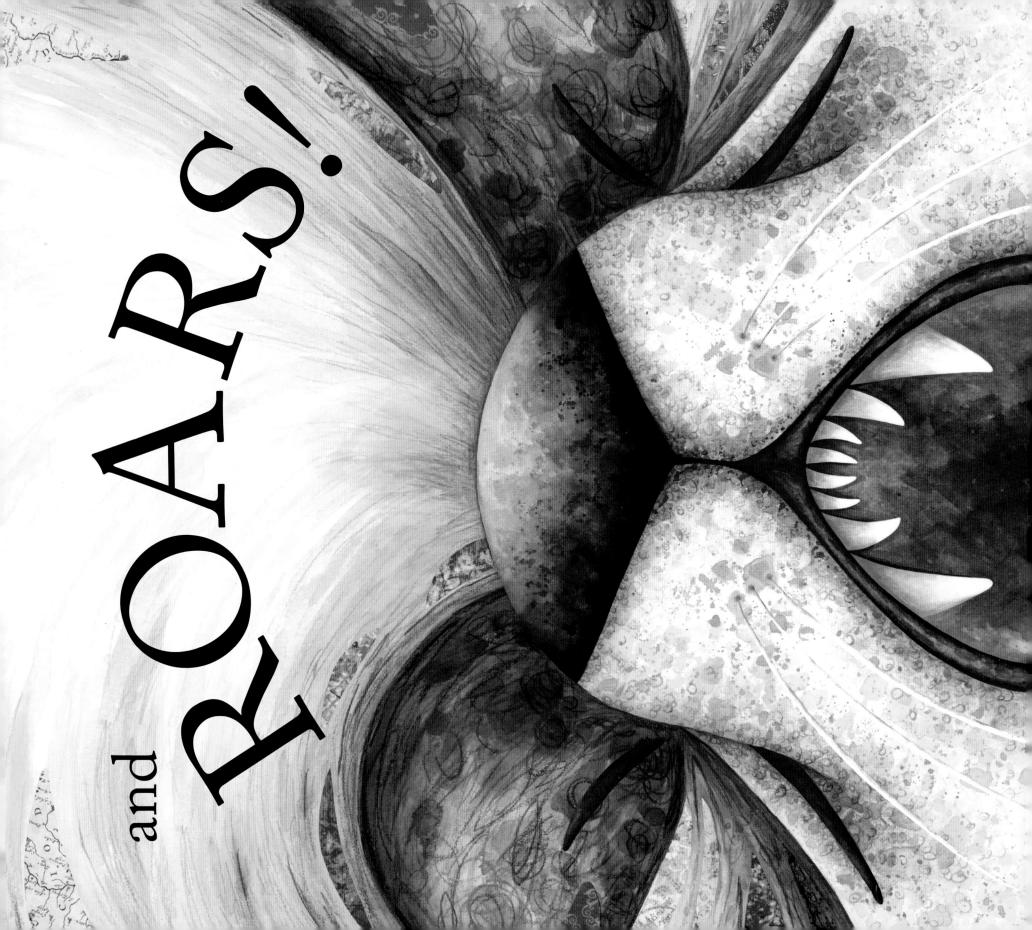

and ROARS!

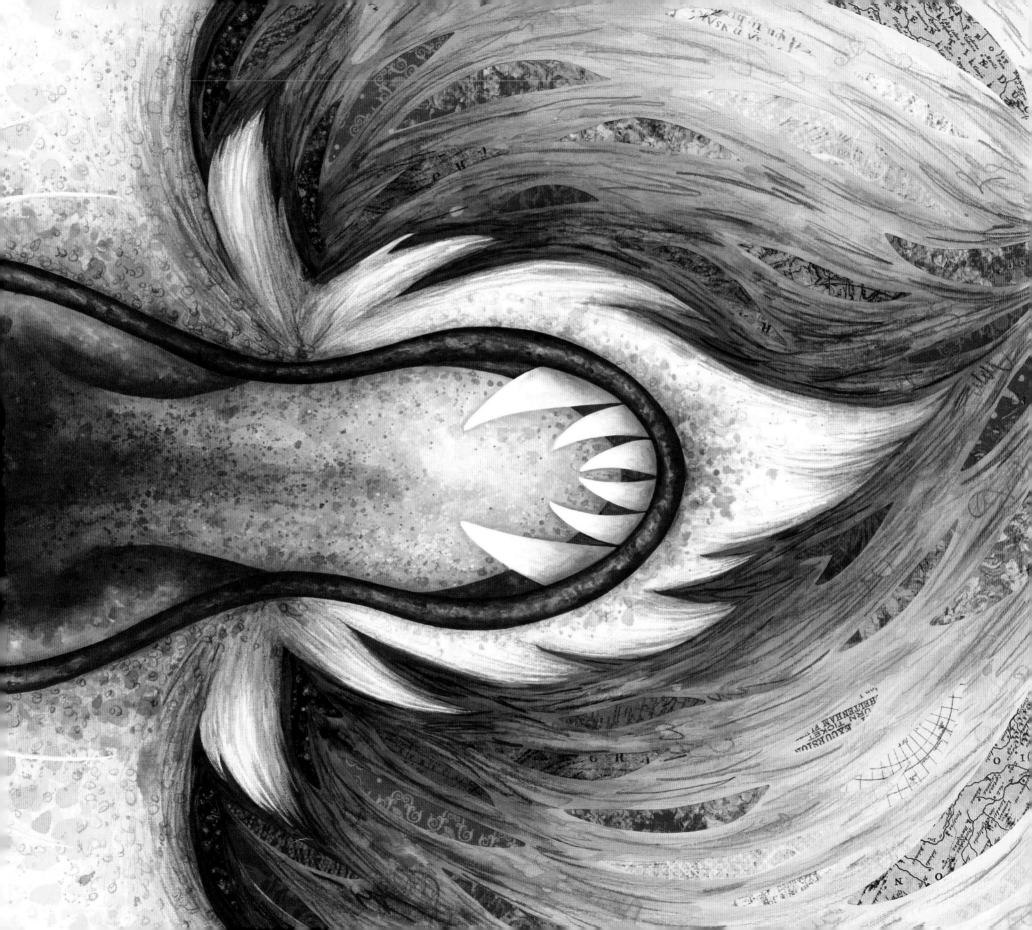

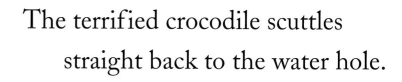

The terrified crocodile scuttles
straight back to the water hole.

"You saved us!" cheer the meerkats.
"But that nasty crocodile took
a big bite out of your mane!"

"Don't worry," says Monty. "My mane is fine as it is. . . ."

"And it's the **perfect** place for my friends to play."